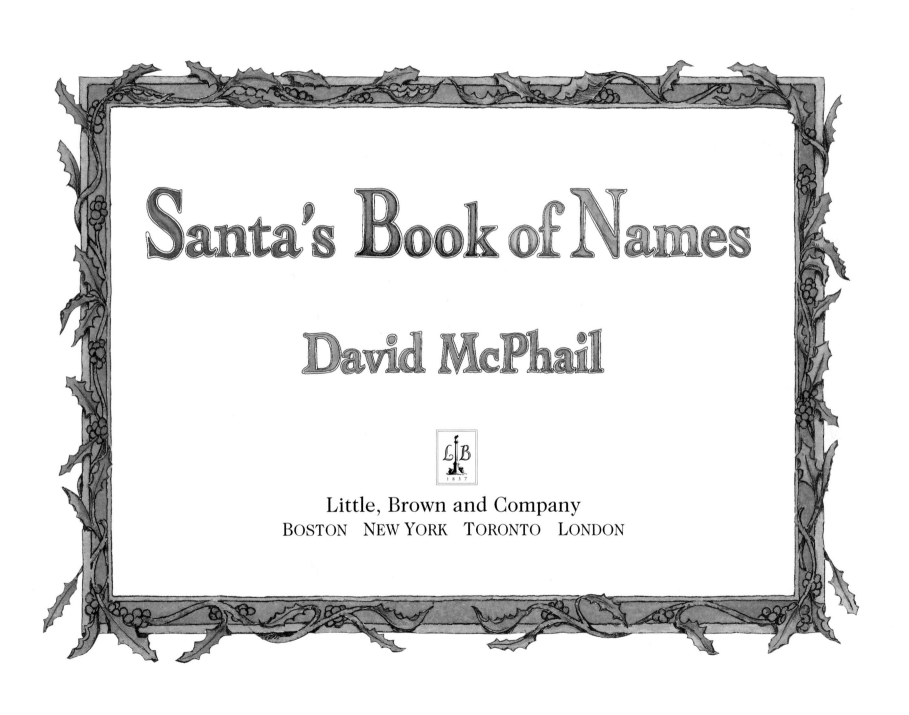

Santa's Book of Names

David McPhail

Little, Brown and Company
BOSTON NEW YORK TORONTO LONDON

**To my mother,
who sang us the songs of Christmas**

Special thanks to Charlene West, first grade teacher
at Greenwood Elementary School, Greenwood, Missouri,
for her advice and counsel.

First Paperback Edition

Library of Congress Cataloging-in-Publication Data

McPhail, David M.
    Santa's book of names / David McPhail. — 1st ed.
        p.   cm.
    Summary: A young boy who has trouble reading helps Santa with his
yearly rounds and receives a special Christmas present.
    ISBN 0-316-11534-7 (pb)
    [1. Reading — Fiction. 2. Santa Claus — Fiction. 3. Christmas —
Fiction.] I. Title.
PZ7.M4788184Sat   1993
[E] — dc20   92-37279

10   9   8   7   6   5   4   3   2

NIL

Published simultaneously in Canada
by Little, Brown & Company (Canada) Limited

Printed in Italy

dward was good at numbers (he could count all the way to fifty). He could recite the alphabet and knew the names of most of the dinosaurs, but when he opened a book and tried to read it, he just couldn't.

Edward's teacher was concerned. She sent a note to Edward's mother and father urging that he be tested to find out what the problem was.

No tests, Edward's mother wrote back. *Patience*.

At bedtime on Christmas Eve, Edward's father read aloud Edward's favorite Christmas story.

In the story, Santa Claus delivers presents to boys and girls around the world.

"How does Santa Claus remember the names of all the boys and girls he gives presents to?" Edward asked when his father had finished. "And where they live? And what toys to bring them?"

"He must have a good memory," said Edward's father.

"Or maybe he has it all written down in a book," said Edward's mother, as she came in to say good night.

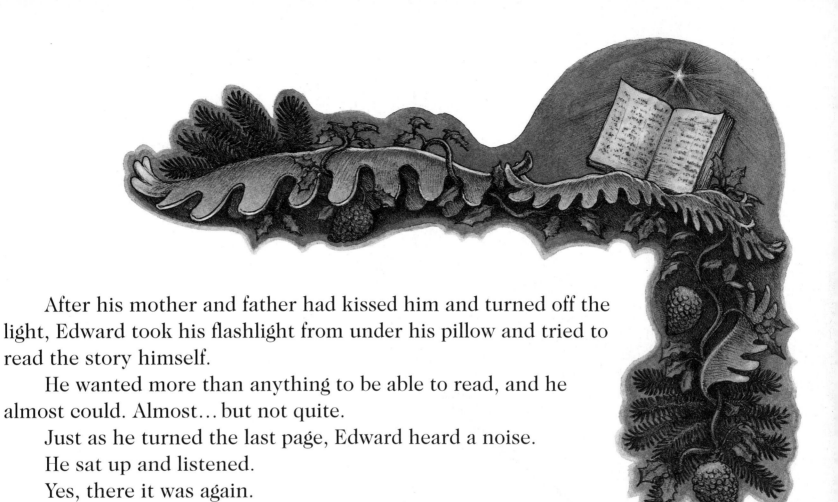

After his mother and father had kissed him and turned off the light, Edward took his flashlight from under his pillow and tried to read the story himself.

He wanted more than anything to be able to read, and he almost could. Almost… but not quite.

Just as he turned the last page, Edward heard a noise.

He sat up and listened.

Yes, there it was again.

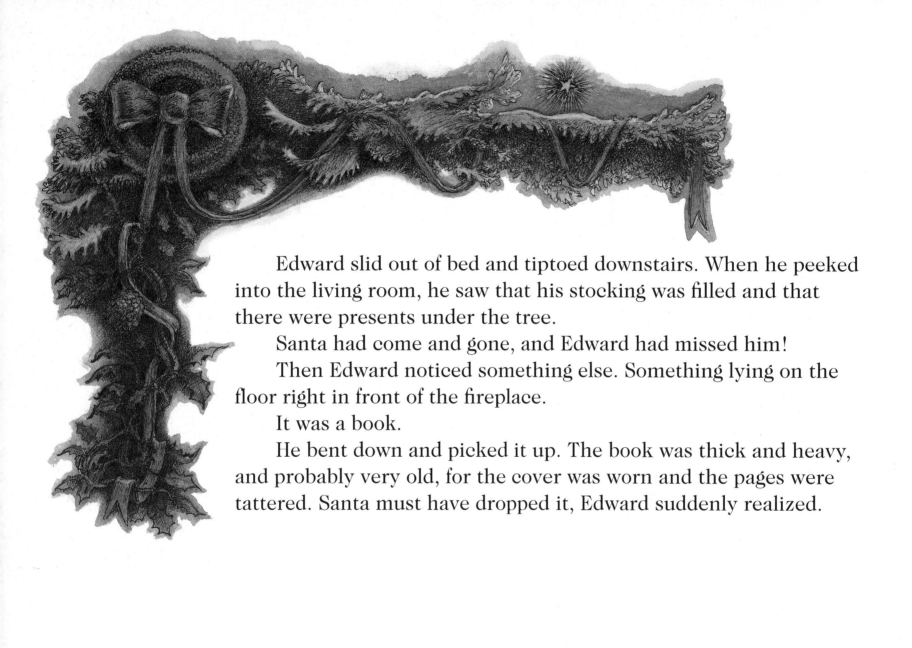

Edward slid out of bed and tiptoed downstairs. When he peeked into the living room, he saw that his stocking was filled and that there were presents under the tree.

Santa had come and gone, and Edward had missed him!

Then Edward noticed something else. Something lying on the floor right in front of the fireplace.

It was a book.

He bent down and picked it up. The book was thick and heavy, and probably very old, for the cover was worn and the pages were tattered. Santa must have dropped it, Edward suddenly realized.

He ran to the front door, threw it open, and stepped outside.

Just as he did, a long shadow passed over him and glided across the fresh, moonlit snow.

"Santa, wait!" cried Edward. "You forgot your book!"

But in the jingle of sleigh bells and the rush of the wind, Santa didn't hear, and in an instant he was gone.

How far could Santa get without his book? Edward wondered. And when Santa realized the book was missing, how would he know where to find it?

Then Edward had an idea.

He hurried back into the house, quickly put on his boots, mittens, coat, and hat.

He knew what letter the word *book* started with, so he tromped out a huge letter *B* in the snow.

Would Santa see it? And even if he did, would he know what it meant?

Then Edward heard the sound of sleigh bells growing closer.

He looked up.

High overhead, Santa's sleigh appeared. It circled once, then went into a steep dive, gliding to a stop right beside Edward.

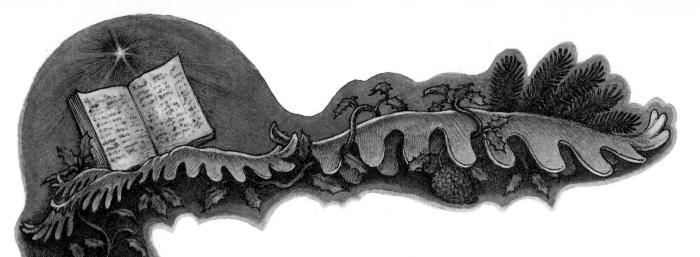

"Hello, Edward. I see that you found my book," said Santa, who looked very much like the Santa in Edward's storybook, except that his nose wasn't round — it was pointed.

"That book contains the names and addresses of all the children in the world," Santa explained. "Most of them I know by heart, but I can't always remember which present to leave. That's why I need my book!"

Edward held the book out to Santa.

"Thank you, Edward," said Santa, and he gently patted Edward's shoulder. "It would be a big help if you would come along and read it to me when I forget something."

Ride with Santa in his sleigh? Edward couldn't believe his ears. He stared down at the glistening snow.

"I — I can't help you, Santa," he stammered. "I can't read."

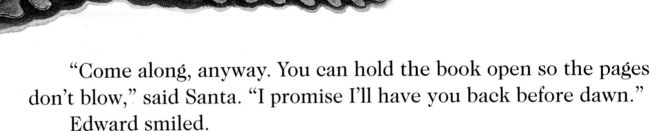

"Come along, anyway. You can hold the book open so the pages don't blow," said Santa. "I promise I'll have you back before dawn."

Edward smiled.

"Okay," he said, and he jumped into the sleigh beside Santa, who bundled him up in thick woolen robes and placed the open book in his lap.

Then Santa gave a low whistle, and the reindeer lunged forward, lifting the sleigh into the crisp, clear air.

From rooftop to rooftop they went. At each stop, Santa would disappear down the chimney with a small bag full of toys.

Presently, they came to a great city. Skyscrapers, dark and silent, loomed around and above them as Santa made his way from one apartment house to the next.

A million children must live in this city, thought Edward, and Santa delivers toys to every one of them. How he did it, Edward couldn't say.

Does time slow down, he wondered — or even stop — on Christmas Eve, while Santa goes about his work?

On they went, to other cities and to every town and village in between. "I'll go wherever there's a child," Santa said.

All this time, Edward had been holding the book and turning the pages so that Santa, his glasses balanced on the end of his nose, could glance over and read what was written beside each name.

He read aloud: "Pablo Lopez…paint set" and "Lucy Wells… baseball mitt," as Edward followed along.

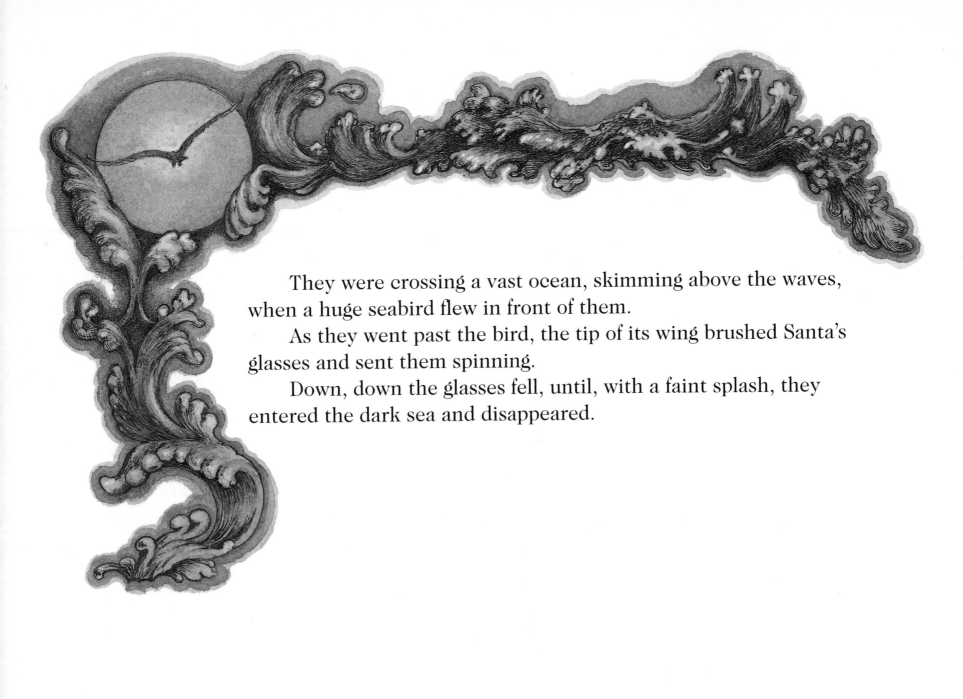

They were crossing a vast ocean, skimming above the waves, when a huge seabird flew in front of them.

As they went past the bird, the tip of its wing brushed Santa's glasses and sent them spinning.

Down, down the glasses fell, until, with a faint splash, they entered the dark sea and disappeared.

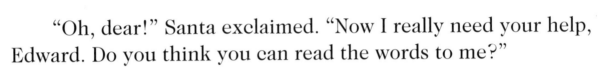

"Oh, dear!" Santa exclaimed. "Now I really need your help, Edward. Do you think you can read the words to me?"

Edward knew Santa was counting on him.

"I'll try," he said.

"Good," said Santa. "I was up to the seventh name on that page: Ben Hill."

Edward counted down the page to number seven. Beside the name was a word that looked familiar to him.

"Buh…buh…," Edward began.

"That's right," Santa said. "Just sound it out."

"Buh…o…o…k," said Edward. "Book!"

"A book it is, then," declared Santa as he landed the sleigh and stepped out.

"What's next, Edward?" Santa asked upon his return.

Edward looked up at Santa. "Dah…doll," he said proudly.

After that, Edward continued to read the words to Santa.

And while Santa was delivering one present, Edward was getting another one ready to go.

Finally they were finished.

Edward closed the *Book of Names* and placed it on the seat beside him as Santa emerged from the last chimney and took one final present from his bag.

It was a book.

"Merry Christmas!" said Santa as he handed the book to Edward. "Thank you for all your help. I couldn't have done it without you."

Then he took up the reins once more, and in an instant they were streaking through the dawning sky.

Edward opened his book to the first page and stared down at the words.

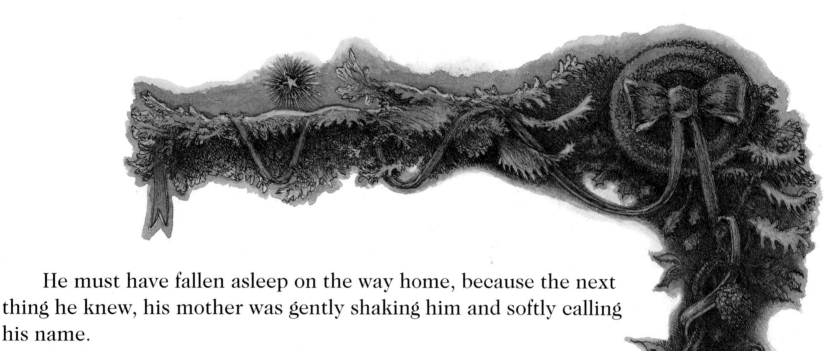

He must have fallen asleep on the way home, because the next thing he knew, his mother was gently shaking him and softly calling his name.

"Merry Christmas, Edward," she whispered. "Time to wake up and see what Santa Claus brought you."

Edward opened his eyes. He was lying on the sofa in front of the fireplace.

"Look at what Santa left you," said Edward's father as he bent down and picked up a book. "Would you like me to read it to you?"

Edward smiled.

"No thanks, Dad," he replied. "Let *me* read it to *you*."

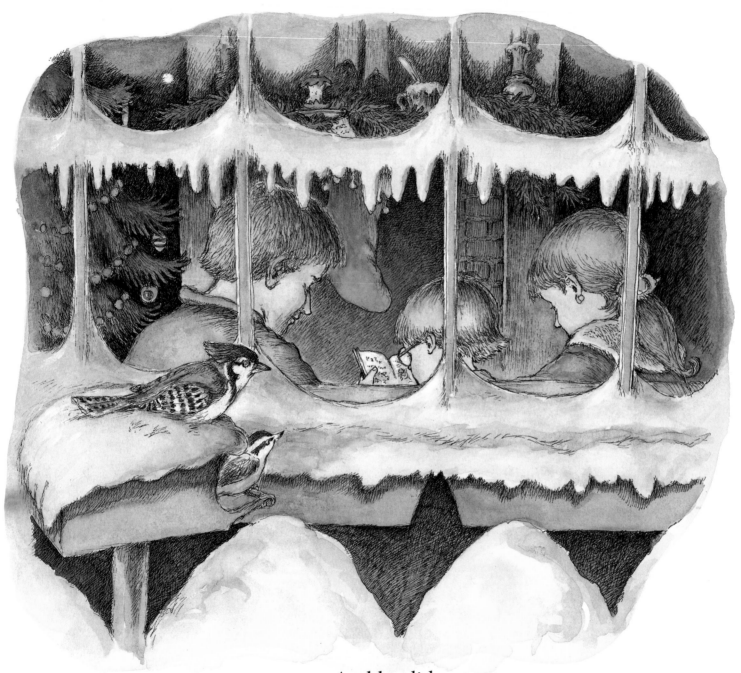

And he did.